Craving

Redemption

The Ways We Heal

Table of Contents

CHAPTER ONE

Hank pulled Daven aside after the sermon, moving him gently into their usual after-church chatting place in the corner of the lobby. It was private there, and Avery stood a discreet distance away to ensure their safety.

"Hank," Daven began as he handed over his boss's phone. "I… I'm so sorry. I hope you're not angry with me."

"Not at all. You were right." He dropped the phone into his pocket, struggling not to laugh again. "No harm done. Speaking of phones, are you going to call Shane about the issues you were having yesterday morning? I want a full report of exactly what went wrong and why your phone was not taking calls for several hours. We know it's not a problem with the emergency line, since Floyd and-"

Hank stopped in surprise as Lucas suddenly approached him. It was highly unusual for any of the guards to interrupt a conversation, especially the aloof and distant Lucas. But he had also drilled into all of his staff that they are never to apologize for doing their job, so the man got straight to the point.

"Sir, the boys were fighting again. I've stopped it, but a lot of people saw it. We need to take them to the car."

Hank sighed. "For fuck's sake. Take Theo, but send Floyd to me."

"*Hank!*" gasped Daven as Lucas walked away.

"Sorry, Dav. Still inside a church, I know."

Daven shook his head. "We shouldn't be speaking in here about party business. Especially not this topic. Is there a good time we can talk today? I have something we need to discuss."

Hank nodded. "Your car outside?"

"Yes."

"Let's go there and talk, then."

"Wait, what about Floyd?"

"Oh...yeah." Hank turned around and watched as his son walked up to him with a "who, me?" expression. Hank wasn't buying it, and he gestured for him to walk with him about ten feet away from Dav.

"Can I trust you to sit in the car with your brother for ten minutes without killing him, or am I going to have to take you into the restroom for a chat?" he asked calmly, with a neutral expression. People were watching, after all. They were *always* watching.

Floyd swallowed hard. A *chat* was never actually a chat in this context.

"Theo keeps making fun of me, dad. I have a right to defend myself."

"Making fun of you? For what?"

Floyd looked at the floor. "For...forget it. I'd rather *have a chat* than explain it. I'll meet you in the restroom."

Hank was bewildered and hurt at his son's attitude. "*Stop*, Floyd," he said as he stepped in front of him to block the path. "What's gotten into you?" he asked harshly. Floyd then looked ready to burst into tears, so Hank put his hands on his son's shoulders and softened his tone. "Hey. Forget it, we'll talk later. Just relax. Let's go to breakfast. Come on."

He put his arm around Floyd and walked back to Daven. "I'll have to call you later, Dav. Floyd isn't feeling well."

With Avery and Daven leading the way, Hank guided his son down to his waiting car. This time, he didn't wave because he forgot the press was even there.

Hank leaned his head into the car. "Hey, Theo. You're going to ride with the guards this morning while I talk to Floyd alone. Come on out."

Theo climbed out, smirking at his miserable brother. Hank saw it and gave him a warning glance, but he still couldn't decipher what was going on between them. He was determined to find out.

It was an hour-long drive to where the Bancroft family had their weekly Sunday brunch with the entire household before the work week started up again. The hotel was located in a poorer section of the city, where most of the servants spent their Saturdays. Every Sunday at 10am Hank rented out a ballroom at the Hilton and had a nice banquet brunch served for the household staff, which was about twenty people, and for their immediate families. It was a rather large affair. A motorcoach was waiting to take the servants back to the house afterwards, but there was no urgent rush to leave since they didn't need to arrive until 3pm to start preparing for dinner.

On Friday nights at 9pm, the same motorcoach arrived at the house and took them into a parking lot in the city where they could be picked up by their families. It was an extremely thoughtful and expensive arrangement, and no one else with such a large household ever did the same for their servants. Hank prided himself on obtaining respect and loyalty by serving up plenty of the same in return. On these days they celebrated birthdays, anniversaries, and promotions for the upcoming week, and Hank always attended even if it meant his travel plans had to be changed. Everyone in the Bancroft household loved Hank and the boys.

The downside was that every Sunday, *everybody* knew where Hank Bancroft and his sons were going to be. That's why their little town car was followed by a van full of security guards -

and this time - Theo, too - even though no one else from the Seditionists party was ever invited.

Hank expected Floyd to resent him for forcing him to ride with him alone and talk about his feelings, but he was pleasantly surprised when the boy scooted up next to him and all but *cuddled* with him. Cuddled. *Floyd* . Cuddling. Something was really wrong.

As he put his arm around his son, Hank asked the driver to close the partition window for privacy. Then he handed Floyd a bottle of his favorite iced tea and lemonade drink. Floyd didn't take it, so Hank set it down. His stomach began growling, and Floyd chuckled.

"Oh you think that's funny, huh?" Hank said with a smirk.

"Yeah. Sorry."

"I know what else you thought was funny today."

Floyd chuckled again, but just barely. "Yeah. Uncle Dav taking your phone away. I wish you could have seen your face, dad. It was hilarious."

"I'm sure it was."

"And his face, too. He was so pissed at you."

"Ha. What else is new."

Silence.

"Does Uncle Dav get mad at you a lot, dad?" Floyd sounded like he was falling asleep.

"Yes. Usually when he thinks I'm acting childish. You know he hates that we don't take church seriously. And sometimes we fight about party policy, but that's only because we care passionately about what we believe in. And we don't always agree on everything, and sometimes we don't talk for a while and act like brats. Just like you and your brother."

Silence.

"So now that I've told you what's going on between me and Dav," Hank said, drawing his son closer to him and running a hand through his hair, "I want you to tell me what's going on between you and Theo, so we can fix it."

Silence.

"Floyd?"

Silence.

"Can you promise me you won't be mad at me for what I'm about to tell you?"

Oh, lovely. What now? "No."

Floyd grumbled, "Never mind, then."

"Talk to me, Floyd," said Hank, a little sterner. "I guarantee you I will be mad if you don't let me in on what's going on between you too."

Floyd sighed. "You're going to find out from Lucas, anyway. I hit him because he was making fun of me for not being able to sit still in church. Because my butt hurt, because of what *he did* yesterday morning. I should have never gone to the office to get you. He's stupid and was just being a big baby, and I don't care about him anymore. He can cry for days for all I care!"

Hank was stunned by Floyd's hostility, both in words and action. "You *hit* him? In the church, you mean, just now?"

"Yeah. Well it was more of a shove, I guess. Kind of."

"What *exactly* did you do?" Hank asked calmly, although his heart was pounding out of his chest.

Silence.

"Floyd. Tell me."

"I...I shoved him. He fell down but he wasn't hurt. I also kind of slapped the back of his head. Lucas saw the whole thing, he can tell you why I did it."

Hank was incensed. "I don't care why, Floyd. You're in serious trouble. You should never, *ever* , hit your brother. Period. I've made this very clear to both of you boys throughout your entire lives. And doing it in public makes it ten times worse."

"But dad-"

"Be quiet. I don't want to hear anymore. Sit up and move to that bench."

Floyd peeled himself off his dad and moved to the lengthwise bench of limousine, where he laid down again. "Dad-"

"Quiet. And sit up straight."

"My butt hurts."

"And it's going to hurt a lot more when we get home. Plant it straight down on that seat or else I'll plant it for you."

Floyd sat up, but he wasn't happy about it. Hank didn't care. He pulled out his BlackBerry and called Daven.

"Yes?"

"It's Hank. Sorry we got interrupted. You talk with Shane yet?"

"Just hung up with him, actually. He's going to look into it. Do you have an hour or so to talk later today? I need to bring something to your attention that could potentially blow up into something much bigger, but I don't want to get into it now while you're on the way to brunch. We may need more than an hour, and it's best if we do it in person."

"It can't wait until tomorrow?"

Daven paused. "Unfortunately not. The sooner, the better. And we should meet at the office."

Hank eyed Floyd, his heart hurting from the fact that his boys had gotten physical with each other. "The office should be fine. I was going to take my son for a driving lesson, but that's just been canceled."

"That reminds me, I don't know if you had a chance to talk to Lucas, but nearly everyone saw that scuffle between your boys."

"I'm sure they did."

"You should call him and get the whole story from him before you take action-"

Hank interrupted him rudely. "Dav, this is not your jurisdiction. End of story. I'll call you when I leave the hotel so we can figure out a time to meet today. About *party business.* Only."

He hung up, feeling furious at Daven now, too. Was everyone out to ruin his day, or what?

Twenty very long and silent minutes later, Hank's phone rang. It was Theo.

"What's up?" Hank asked quietly, not wanting Floyd to know it was Theo for fear of a temper tantrum. The boy suspected nothing and barely glanced at him with his red eyes that were still wet but no longer spouting tears.

"Is Floyd okay, dad?"

"Yeah, why do you ask?"

There was a long pause. "Because I feel really bad about what I did, and he was right to be mad. I just feel really bad and I want to talk to him."

Hank's heart dropped. "What exactly did you do?" he asked in a business-like tone.

"He didn't tell you?"

"Nope. Maybe it's best if I hear it from you."

An even longer pause. Floyd's eyes were closed now, but his face was white and he was clenching his fists harder than before.

"I knew you took a belt to him and I was making fun of him for not being able to sit still during the sermon. Because it hurt. As we were leaving the church I picked up a bible and...." there was a choking noise and a cry and at least a minute of nothing else.

Then another voice on the phone. Lucas. "You want me to finish the story for him, Mr. Bancroft? He's lost it again."

"Yes, please go ahead," said Hank tightly, gritting his teeth with keen distaste. The last thing he wanted was his guards involved in the family's personal business.

"As we were exiting he picked up the bible and with both hands took a huge swing at Floyd's rear. Hit him pretty hard. Floyd turned around and pushed him away, and Theo fell. Lost his balance, I think, it wasn't a very hard shove."

Jesus Christ. "And then what?"

"Floyd smacked Theo in the back of the head, not hard, told him to stop. Then Theo picked up the bible again and went after Floyd as he started down the stairs, and nearly hit him with it again but I managed to grab him back by the collar. I'm sorry to tell you almost everyone saw and heard it. There was some commentary afterwards in the lobby, which is why I interrupted your conversation with Mr. Johansson.”

Now Hank felt like crying, out of frustration and anger. “I see. Objectively, who would you consider to be at fault in this situation?”

“Theo, no question. It was unprovoked, and Floyd was trying to get away rather than fight.”

Hank took a deep breath. “Okay. Thanks. We’ll see you at the hotel.”

He disconnected the call, then stared at Floyd placidly until he opened his eyes and turned to look. His heart fell when Floyd shied away from him, moving further up the bench.

“Come here, Floyd.” He patted the bench gently. “That was Theo and Lucas. I know what Theo did, and you’re off the hook. You can lay down.” He scooted over the far left to give Floyd room to stretch out, but Floyd didn’t move. He looked like the proverbial deer caught in the headlights.

“I’m okay here,” he whispered.

Hank waited, but Floyd stayed put. So he got up and clambered over the other bench next to Floyd and wrapped his arms gently around his son and kissed his forehead.

"I'm sorry I didn't let you explain. That was wrong. Next time, I will. I always will from now on. I promise. Okay?"

Floyd sniffled, then nodded. He was a lot more upset than Hank realized, and it was going to take a while for him to recover. Hank was infinitely glad he chose not to spank him in the limo again a little while ago.

A few minutes later, when Floyd was quiet again, Hank let him lay down and put his head in his lap. Then he ran his hand through his hair slowly, gently.

"Floyd?"

"Yeah, dad?"

Hank was a little choked up suddenly. "Yesterday, when you called me a crappy father…"

Floyd started to sit up. "I didn't mean it, I'm so sorry!"

Hank pressed him back down. "Listen. Even if you didn't, you're weren't entirely wrong. I've been thinking, you know? It killed me that you said that, but I needed to know you felt that way. I heard you, loud and clear. And I'm going to be a better father and spend a lot more time with you guys. You have my word."

Floyd said nothing. He was trembling again, and his eyes were closed.

"I can't take back anything I've done or haven't done," Hank continued. "So all that resentment you have towards me is just going to linger unless you let it go on your own free will, when you're ready. I hope it's sooner than later, but I wouldn't blame you if it's never. God forbid."

"What are you going to do to Theody?" Floyd asked quietly.

"First I'm going to paddle the daylights out of him, and then I'm going to have this same talk with him. He won't be very receptive to it, of course, but that's Theo. We'll have to see how it goes. Take it day by day."

Floyd murmured, "You should talk to him first. And *then* paddle him. He learns better that way. Opposite of me."

Hank nodded, impressed with Floyd's sudden wisdom. Why hadn't he himself ever picked up on that distinction before? "You're exactly right. I'll do that. Speaking of which, how's your rear?"

"Hurts."

"I'm sorry. You didn't deserve what Theo did."

Floyd asked hopefully, "Does this mean my driving lesson is back on again?"

Hank laughed. "Yeah, I suppose so. Remind me to have a few drinks beforehand."

Floyd didn't laugh, but he visibly relaxed. After a moment Hank took his hand and squeezed it.

Floyd squeezed back and didn't let go.

They were silent the rest of the way to the hotel.

CHAPTER TWO

Hank was always the last out of the limo when the little caravan arrived at the Hilton, per his bodyguard's wishes. The hotel was kind enough to always offer a private parking area covered by a tent so that the press couldn't hound his every step into the hotel. That's part of the reason Hank was fine with giving them so much money week after week.

"Vance," Hank called out to his driver, who had exited on the other side of the car and was now scurrying around to meet his boss.

"Sir?"

"I need you to take Theo home and stay there. Floyd and I will ride back with the guards. But first go inside the ballroom and eat something; he'll wait for you here."

Vance nodded and disappeared, and Hank grabbed Theo's arm and guided him over to the limo.

"Get in," ordered Hank quietly. The guards that were all standing around waiting for him to enter the hotel looked puzzled, as did Floyd, but Hank ignored them all and climbed into the car after Theo and shut the door behind him.

"You have no idea how much trouble you're in, do you?" Hank asked calmly.

Theo was trembling, just like Floyd had been an hour ago. "I think I know. You're sending me home so I can wait in the spare room for you, and then...then you're going to...."

Hank nodded. "You can go to the kitchen for a bottle of water first, *only,* and then straight to the spare room. Except for calls of nature you will stay in there until I return home. And then yes, I'm *going to.* Big time."

He got out of the car and told Avery to stay with it until Vance returned. Then he gestured everybody else inside the hotel with him, and everyone put on their happy faces for the next couple of hours.

The ride home in the van was completely silent because Hank had received a phone call during breakfast that put him in a scary, snappy mood. Floyd could barely dare to blink after having received a solid smack on the butt for taking too long to leave the ballroom - given right in front of all the guards and some of the hotel staff, no less. Floyd was so humiliated and angry that Avery felt obliged to take him aside to calm him down, and then Hank went after Avery for that, too. When the subdued contingent finally piled into the van, Floyd jumped in first and scrambled to the very back to keep at a safe distance from his irate father.

Floyd had no idea what was upsetting his dad so much. It was extremely rare for him to be so bossy with his guards, and until now he had never once disciplined his kids in public. They were all rather bewildered by the whole affair, but it became clearer once they pulled up to the house and spotted Daven's truck in the driveway.

Hank was the first out of the van.

"I told you I would meet you at the office!" he snapped so loudly that everyone cringed.

Daven responded calmly, "I told you this can't wait. We can drive there together if you want, but-"

"No. My study. Go in. I'll be right there. Floyd!"

"Yes, dad?" answered Floyd in a small voice, and Hank spun around to see his son standing right behind him.

"Go straight to your room and stay there until I tell you to come out. Understand?"

Floyd felt like crying again. "You're scaring me. What's going on?"

"When I tell you to move, you move. Or do you need another reminder?" He raised his hand.

"No!" Floyd ran off, and Hank turned to his four-person security contingent, who were standing in a square around him, looking extremely concerned.

"Everything alright, boss?" ventured Avery in a neutral tone.

"Not even close, but it's not a security matter. Sorry for being an ass. You can return to quarters and relax. I'll call down when I'm ready to go back out."

Hank said nothing more and turned around to go in the house. He held the door open so the guards could go down the stairs to their rooms, then headed straight for the spare room in order to let Theo know he would be a little while longer. He was shocked to find Floyd sitting on the bed next to his brother; the boy jumped up immediately and began apologizing.

Hank was furious. "I said go *straight* to your room. Was I unclear in any way whatsoever, Floyd?"

"Theo's hungry, dad. We've been gone for-"

"Out. Now!"

Hank forgot all about what he was going to tell Theo and followed Floyd out, slamming the door behind them. Then he made a beeline for his study, where his chief strategist was standing there looking like a man who just ran over his best friend's dog.

"*Daven,*" he growled as he strode in and set his briefcase hard down on the table. "There better be a really good fucking explanation for the information we just received from Shane. Start talking."

"Maybe you should calm down first," tried Dav, but Hank wasn't having it.

"Did you, or did you not, *deliberately* turn off your phone while we were waiting for the agent's call to come through on the emergency line?"

"Hank, I know you're upset, but please listen to me first. It's complicated."

"I only want a yes or no answer. *Now*."

Daven took a deep breath to steady himself. "Yes."

Hank shook his head in disbelief. "Alright. You're fired, then. Whatever you choose to tell me at this point is on your own time."

"I'm certainly not going to talk to you while you're this upset," Daven finally declared, firmly but somewhat breathlessly.

"Did Rupert know about this?" Hank demanded angrily.

"Yes...he figured it out when the alleged agent called him directly after he couldn't reach me."

Hank did not expect that answer at all, and it threw him for a loop. His heart fell even further.

"Wonderful. So you were both conspiring against me. On Christmas. Thanks a lot."

Daven flipped open his notebook. "No, actually. We were both doing our jobs. Our charter has a clause in it which clearly states that all-"

"I have that fucking charter memorized, Dav. Don't quote my own words to me."

"Sorry," replied Daven, truly chagrined. He flipped the notebook shut. "When you are calm, I will explain everything. Do you want me to leave until then?"

"Just a minute," said Hank as he walked over to the intercom on the wall and hit a switch.

"Theo?"

There was a short pause, then Theo's small, tremulous voice. "Yes, dad?"

"You can come out now. Make yourself lunch, then go outside with Floyd and play with the dogs. I'm going to be with Dav for a while, then your brother and I are going for a drive. After that, you and I will talk."

"Yes, sir," replied Theo shakily. "I'm sorry, dad."

"I know. Try to relax, buddy," Hank said softly. "We'll get through this. See you in a bit."

"Okay." Theo's relief was obvious, and Hank smiled a little. To be eleven years old again...

"Oh, Theo? Can you bring me a couple bottles of water to the study first?"

"Sure, dad. Be right there."

While waiting, Hank took out his copy of the charter from his desk and ran his fingers over it without seeing any of the words. They had all written it together, ten years ago. When everything seemed exciting and right and purposeful and pure...but now, not so much. How fast life moved sometimes. Yesterday had been normal. Today, Daven had to be dealt with, and then Rupert. It was all over.

Theo delivered the water, and then it was time.

"You better start from the beginning. This time, don't leave anything out. No opinions, just facts. I am calm and will listen in silence until you finish." He sat down and looked up at his friend - former friend? - expectantly.

Daven took a deep breath. "Very well. On Christmas eve, just after I arrived at your house for the party, I received a call on the emergency line..."

"...and then last night at 9pm, Rupert called me to tell me everything the agent had told him, which was exactly what he told me. But the man still refused to give his code number. At that point we made the decision that the alleged agent was untrustworthy and you needed to be informed of the situation immediately, in case there was a plot against you."

"Except it wasn't immediately."

"No," explained Daven patiently. "We hung up at midnight last night. Remember this morning I told you we needed to get together in person today? Had I known Shane would beat me to the punch with the findings about my phone, I never would have waited. Now it looks like I'm covering my tracks, but I'm not."

Hank was calming down, but Daven was still fired. So very, very fired.

"And how exactly do you expect me to believe you?"

Daven pulled out his phone. "I took measures to ensure you knew Rupert and I were aligned and aware of the seriousness of our actions. Here is an email from me to Rupe at one o'clock this morning with the draft of the memo I wrote you for this very meeting. Here's the final version, sent at 2am. A copy of which is right here in my hand, by the way, signed by both of us and time-stamped at 6:24 this morning. The original is on your desk right now. You can check our badges. We left the office at 6:50am and have not been back again today. I also FedEx'd a copy to your home after leaving the church, which was dropped off at 8:37am. Here's the tracking number."

Hank took all the papers, but said nothing.

"Furthermore," added Daven, "once the decision was made to inform you of our actions, we both wrote our resignations in order to save time. Also time-stamped from this morning and left on your desk."

Hank still said nothing.

Daven continued patiently, "What this all means, Hank, is that Rupert and I took all these actions hours before we even *asked* Shane to start an investigation. So if you still think I'm backtracking now, there's nothing else I can do to convince you otherwise."

"Very thorough," murmured Hank. He didn't want to admit he was impressed, but he was. "I just have one question. Did you know that Shane would be able to tell you turned your phone off? Because one could say you knew you were screwed and are trying to score points by turning yourself in before he had the chance."

"Absolutely not. I was stunned to learn this morning that he was able to do that. Believe me, if I had known *that*, I would've never done it in the first place."

Hank nodded. "Okay. I believe you. Anything else to add?"

Daven took another deep breath. "I'm not trying to get out of being fired, Hank. I accept responsibility for my actions. I should have never turned off my phone, and found another way to speak to the agent. But before I go, I need to say one thing. Your refusal to give me the list of people you met with last Tuesday was the impetus for my decision to keep the details of the call from you. You should have given me the list so I could validate who you're meeting with. That's my job. Or *was*, rather. I would like to know why you wouldn't cooperate with me on that."

Hank was annoyed again. "Because I didn't want to deal with it on Christmas eve. I was tired. I was drunk. I was busy hosting a huge party in my house. The only other person who had access to those names was my secretary, and she was here partying and drunk, too. It had to wait. End of story. Any further questions? Maybe you also want to know what my agent was doing in Greeley when she was killed? Ask Rupert, it was his idea. I'm guessing he didn't tell you that, huh?"

Daven said nothing. What could he possibly say that wouldn't increase Hank's defensiveness and make things worse?

Hank suddenly made up his mind and spoke with a firmness and finality that Daven always appreciated, even if others didn't.

"I don't want to see you again for 30 days. That's how long I'm suspending you. Two weeks for the phone stunt and another two for speaking with an unverified asset. Rupert will also get two weeks for the latter. All unpaid, of course. I'll call him in a moment to tell him."

Daven stared at him in disbelief. "You're not accepting our resignations?"

"Oh, I want to, believe me. But you know I can't. It would destabilize the party and throw our constituents into a frenzy. We're going to have to get through this together and learn how to trust each other again. If possible. I'm not sure how. Time will tell. Give me your BlackBerry and your office badge. You'll get them back on January 25."

Daven handed the objects over.

"I'm so sorry, Hank-"

"*Don't*. Just leave. You're not to have contact with anyone at our office except me and Rupert, and try to keep that to the bare minimum while I stave off the press for the next month. Go."

Daven left the house without another word and drove straight to Rupert's house, his bodyguard faithfully tailing him at a discreet distance.

CHAPTER THREE

Rupert had received the grim news of his fate from Hank directly by the time Daven's truck pulled up the drive, followed by the little dark blue BMW that always accompanied him. He was upset, yet grateful not to have been fired, but was more than a little uneasy about all the unanswered questions and implications that had spent two days raining down on his head in a cycle of nothingness and frustration.

It was likely the agent was a plant...but how did he get the emergency number?

- So it's one of our own agents, since all the others are accounted for.

What if the agent is working with the Urbanes in a plot against Hank?

- What would be the purpose? Hank is free of scandal and on cordial terms with Harmon.

Who would want to kill a double agent on Seditionists territory?

- Maybe it was one of our own who thought she was spying. But there were no reports of that.

If Hank is innocent, why would he not turn over the names of who he met with?

- Remember that Hank has a lot going on in the background that you don't know about.

We shouldn't have speculated at all until this guy was verified.

- We couldn't just leave it alone until he called again. We were obliged to investigate.

...and so on. And so on. And so on.

It was all driving him crazy.

"Sorry to show up unannounced," Daven said apologetically as Rupert opened the door and stepped onto the porch. "Hank took my phone and your number was in there. I don't have it memorized. Do you have time to talk?"

"I do, but he's actually on his way here to take my phone and badge, too. Might make things awkward."

"Oh. Then I'll call you on your home phone later. I need to write it down, though."

Daven pulled out a notebook and took down the number as Rupert read it out, then turned around as Rupe's eyes focused on something else over his shoulder. Daven heard it before he saw it; the noisy Thunderbird roaring down the street, being dutifully tailed by a comically large and shiny black Escalade that wallowed and swayed over the speed bumps like a drunken hippo. As they pulled up, Floyd waved from behind the wheel. The men quickly walked down to the car where it was parking in the street due to Daven's truck and the BMW blocking the driveway.

"Hey Floyd," Rupert called after the engine was shut off. "Looking good, buddy!"

"Hi guys," he replied with a huge grin, but he stayed put. His dad had clearly told him not to get out of the car, or else he would have already been out and giving hugs to his "uncles."

Hank unfolded himself out of the passenger side, then walked up to Rupert without a single glance at Daven. "The house looks good. I like the new color scheme."

"Thanks. The shutters are going to be repainted a shade lighter, though. Came out a bit too dark. And did you notice the driveway?"

Hank looked down at the fresh black asphalt. "Yeah. Looks great. I need to do mine before I sell." He pointed up. "You re-did the chimney, too? Man. Decorative brickwork and everything. Going all out, aren't you."

"Yeah. Got to keep up with all the new money folks rushing into the neighborhood." They both grinned. He meant Hank himself, of course, who had bought the largest plot of land in the neighborhood last year and was almost finished with his new house. The exterior was barely started before all the neighbors started getting catty about it making their own homes look shabby in comparison, and Hank thought it was hilarious that Rupe's own wife was one of the original chief naysayers. That was before she knew it was Hank's. Now everyone knew, of course, because the press had gotten a hold of the building permits.

Daven shifted uncomfortably from where he was observing the disturbingly normal interaction, feeling a bit like he had entered the metaphorical Twilight Zone. But then he spotted Rupe's wife and teenaged children watching from the living room windows, just barely visible behind the glare of noon sunlight. That explained it. Hank had seen them, too, and was being painfully careful to do nothing to alarm them. Or Floyd, for that matter, who had all the windows down in the car and was also watching the scene intently. It was also extremely likely that one or more of the cars on the street had a photographer lying in wait behind the tinted windows, hoping to get a juicy shot to sell.

To that end, Rupert handed his badge and BlackBerry to Hank in two regular envelopes. "See you in two weeks then?" he said lightly, but respectfully.

"At the office, yes. But I still expect you in church on Sunday. *Every* Sunday. Don't skip it again." He was highly annoyed that he had been forced to unfailingly attend per Rupe's insistence, but Rupe didn't always go himself. Like today. If Hank had to suffer, they would all suffer, period.

"Okay. Sorry. Shall I call you at 6pm, or will you call me?"

"I'll call you."

Daven wanted Hank to say something to him, too, but Hank turned back and got into the car, completely ignoring him as if he wasn't even there. Floyd waved again as he pulled out and drove off, and Daven waved back. Hank was watching him coldly through the side mirror.

"Wow," Rupe said gravely, "looks like he is a lot more pissed at you than me. What happened?"

"Sentenced to 4 weeks of being a non-entity, apparently." Daven was wildly depressed all of a sudden, and Rupert felt terribly sorry for him. The usual envy and friendly rivalry he felt toward the man who was best friends with Hank Bancroft dusted away like it was never there to begin with.

"I'm sorry, Dav. Give him time. It'll be alright."

"Why are you two talking tonight?" asked Daven. "Just curious."

"I'm the PR guy, remember? He asked me to write a few paragraphs to explain to the press what happened and wants it by 6pm."

"What are you going to say?"

"That the Seditionists hold all of their party's employees to the same standards, and that we violated a longstanding communications policy. No tolerance even at the highest levels of leadership. Blah blah blah. I'm not exactly sure how to word it yet without ruining our careers. He wants it to be completely transparent, of course. Now I'll also need to explain why you got a bigger punishment than I did. Any ideas?"

"No idea," grumbled Daven. "The Urbanes are going to have a field day with this no matter what we say. I'm so sorry, by the way, for getting you dragged into this. If I hadn't...well, this is all my fault."

"If it helps, neither Hank nor I blame you for my part in this. I spoke with the caller without getting his code first. That was on me."

"Yeah, but if I hadn't ignored his calls, he never would have gotten to you. I resigned, you know, but he wouldn't accept it."

Rupert shrugged. "Yes, Dav, I know. So did I, remember? We literally sat down and wrote our letters together." He shivered.

"It's cold out here. Let's talk later, okay? Try not to mope. It could have been so much worse."

"Not by much."

Rupe looked up, waved up towards his house, and sighed. "Hey, lunch is ready, my wife just waved me in. We can put on an extra plate for you. Why don't you come up? Been a long time since we had the pleasure of your company."

Daven shook his head. "Won't be very pleasurable today, I can assure you. But thanks."

"Nah, I think it's exactly what you need. It's my youngest's birthday today, and we just got a dog. Come in and take your mind off all this. At least for an hour. Come on, Dav. They'll be so happy to see you. And I'll have one of my guards follow you back."

"If you're sure?" Dav asked hopefully. Despite his outward reluctance, he desperately wanted to go in and try to enjoy himself before the shit hit the fan with the press. There was nothing to be gained by going home alone to sit around and think about what a mess he'd made of his friendship with Hank.

"Yeah. Come on. Tell your guard."

"Okay. Be right there."

Daven waited a minute for Rupe to go into the house, and then he walked up to the little BMW and knocked on the window. Gordon rolled it down quickly.

"Yes, boss?"

"You can go on home. Rupe's going to have his guard follow me back."

"I can't, sir, it's against the policy."

"I know. Do it anyway. I'll sign a variance form."

Gordon pulled the stack of forms from beneath the seat behind him. He was the only person in the party who used them on a regular basis, because Daven was constantly violating security and transportation protocol. The signed form completely waived the guard's responsibility for whatever happened once it was signed. Gordon used to protest more in the past at being told to leave his boss all kinds of places alone, but now he was quietly resigned to the fact that nobody at HQ really cared that their chief strategist had very little regard for his own personal safety.

Hank should have been paying more attention to Floyd's driving than he was, but he just couldn't focus. Didn't notice the rolled-through stop sign, blowing a short yellow light, and overall lack of signaling. Didn't notice that the Escalade had to commit the same infractions just to keep up with them. He only sat back and told Floyd to slow down or speed up when he needed to. His mind was elsewhere. Completely, totally dissociated from his current task of ensuring his son didn't kill anybody from behind the wheel of the Thunderbird for the past two hours.

He was already regretting being so hard on Daven, and wished he could take back a few things he'd said. The man was loyal to his party to a fault, and Hank knew he really thought he was doing the right thing. If only he hadn't violated two clear policies, Hank could have let him off easier. If he hadn't talked to the agent. If he hadn't turned off his phone.

And that was the big one - turning off his phone. Daven was the emergency contact for all 50 of their agents. The *only* emergency contact they had. It had been a highly irresponsible and indefensible action to shut that channel down, something that anyone one else would have been fired on the spot for, and probably sued into oblivion for good measure.

Hell, maybe he *should* still fire him for that. But he didn't know, and every five minutes his feelings changed on the matter. It was so frustrating. At this particular moment, he just wanted to strangle the man for putting him in a position to mistrust him.

As if he had been reading his mind, the cell phone rang. It was Rupert's home phone number.

Hank sighed heavily. One of the two people in the world he least wanted to talk to, calling him now in the middle of his son's driving lesson. He should let it go to voicemail.

"Floyd, pull over into this parking lot. Leave room for Avery behind us."

Floyd obeyed, and Hank picked up the call at the last second before it went to voicemail.

"Yes, Rupert?" he answered tensely.

"It's Daven. Do you have a moment?"

Fuck, really? We're doing this right now?

"What do you want, Dav?" he asked irritably, noticing Floyd raising his eyebrows out of the corner of his eye. They both knew he had never spoken to Dav so rudely before. And Hank hated himself for it, but he couldn't help it.

"I just realized the emergency line is still routed to my phone. Shane needs to forward it to someone else as soon as possible, until I come back."

You mean *if I let you* come back, Hank thought to himself.

"Who do you suggest?" he asked, forcing himself to be diplomatic now that Daven had just saved Hank's own ass from charges of neglecting the emergency line. *Jesus Christ, Hank.*

"Taylor."

"I will call Shane right now and arrange it. Thank you for reminding me."

He hung up before Daven could say anything else, then dialed Shane.

"Mr. Bancroft?"

"Sorry to bother you. I need you to re-route the emergency line to Taylor right away. Like yesterday."

There was a clicking of keyboard keys that lasted about 20 seconds.

"Shane..?"

"One moment."

Hank glanced sideways at Floyd, who was watching him with an expression of alarm. This was exactly why he never took work calls around his sons.

"It's done, sir. I take it that means you received my report this morning?"

Oh good god, he had never written Shane back. The poor guy must still be... *shit.*

"Um, yes. Are you still at the office waiting for us?"

"Yes, sir. That's what I was told to do, in case you had more questions."

More than six hours ago. Jesus Christ, Hank. You seriously need to get your shit together.

"Shane...fuck. I'm so sorry. Go home. I'll add an extra vacation day to your file. Make it two, and I'll buy you lunch tomorrow. I'm really sorry." His face burned with embarrassment. Goddamnit. Daven or Rupert would have picked up on this if they hadn't been so busy screwing up everything else.

"No problem, sir. It's good I was still here because I couldn't have made the change to the emergency line from home. Does Taylor know about this so she can keep her phone on? I'm seeing it's turned off right now."

"Okay, thanks. I'll call her at home or on her wife's cell. Good work, Shane."

"Thank you, sir."

Hank hung up and Floyd turned to him immediately.

"Dad? What the hell is going on?"

"Just a moment, Floyd," Hank said as movement in the rearview mirror caught his eye. The Escalade idling behind them was now pulling out to the right and sidling up to his door, looming so large that Hank had to look way up at the driver.

"Everything alright, sir?" asked Avery, looking down at him worriedly. "We're not in a great part of town right now and I'd really like to get you headed back the other way."

"Okay. I need a minute to make an emergency call, and then let's head straight home. I want everyone assembled in the conference room downstairs and waiting for us when we pull in."

"Everyone? Theo, too?"

"No, sorry. I mean just the security team. And wait a sec, Floyd's going to join you for the ride back."

Hank turned to Floyd now and said gently, "I have to make a call that you can't be allowed to hear. Go hop in with Avery."

"Dad, you're seriously freaking me out. I ran two stop signs in a row just to see if you'd notice, and you said nothing. You're not even here right now."

Hank hardened his tone. "I do *not* have time for this, Floyd. I'm in the middle of handling an emergency. Get out of the car, now."

Floyd was becoming slightly hysterical. "No. I'm not going until you tell me what's up. I'm freaking out. What happened with Rupe and Uncle Dav? Are they okay? Are we in danger?"

Lucas appeared on the driver side to open the door, but Floyd quickly jammed down the lock.

Losing control of his temper now, Hank smoothly dragged Floyd out of the passenger side of the car, then gently but firmly pinned him against the side of the SUV. He was furious, but kept his tone level and low.

"That's it. You're getting the belt again. I can do it right here over the trunk of the car, or you can get in the SUV immediately and I'll do it at home. You choose."

"You wouldn't do it here," Floyd challenged. "It would be bad publicity."

"I don't see any cameras around here, do you? I'll give you three seconds to decide. One. Two."

"Home!" Floyd blurted, and Hank immediately loosened his grip.

Floyd scrambled away and fled for safety in the far back row of the giant SUV. Hank followed him and stood at the door, glaring at him while he buckled in. Once that was done, Hank slammed the door and stalked off to his car to call Taylor.

The guards said absolutely nothing, of course, and kept their eyes carefully averted away from Floyd. But it was clear what they were all thinking: they sympathized with Hank, but they also felt really sorry for Floyd, too.

Hank was finally calming down as he made his way from the spare room downstairs into the conference room, where all his guards were waiting to hear exactly what the hell was going on with their boss. He had to talk fast; the servants were due back from Eagle Rock at any moment. He looked around to confirm all nine guards were present, and then immediately launched into his explanation.

"I can't give too many details, gentlemen and lady, but the short story is that my leadership team experienced a major hiccup today and we've lost Rupert for two weeks, and Daven for a month, for disciplinary reasons. So my workload just tripled, and I'll be working 24/7 and traveling around to meetings everywhere. It's likely the Urbanes will take every chance they get to follow me around more closely, and will likely be spying a little extra on the boys as well. Not to mention all of you, in order to monitor my movements. We all need to up our game and make things seem as normal as possible until this blows over. It should hit the news tomorrow morning. Any questions?"

Avery spoke up, as he always did. He was extremely good at his job but never failed to bring up particularly painful points of discussion. Hank didn't hold it against him, though. He had never been out of line even once with his concerns.

"This is obviously going to put a lot of stress on Floyd and Theo, as well. Do you expect to spend all day in the office now, and how do you want us to handle them if they start acting out while you're not here? With all the fighting lately, it may become a problem and there might be a point where they have to be disciplined on the spot before things get too carried away."

There was a slight uncomfortable murmur of agreement among the guards, and Hank groaned internally. Again, a painful point. More so than usual. But absolutely necessary.

"Yeah, thanks Avery for bringing that up." Hank chuckled lightly, and the guards followed suit and relaxed a little. "The boys are...well, for those of you who haven't already heard, they were fighting in church today in front of the entire congregation. I'm sure it's going to be gleefully reported in the papers tomorrow that Hank Bancroft's bodyguards had step in to keep his sons from killing each other."

He stopped in order to gauge the reaction from the guards, who looked alternately horrified and embarrassed. Just like Hank felt, actually.

Hank took a deep breath. "Look, I'm just as uncomfortable talking about this as you are to hear it. But Avery brought up a good point. With the boys being on winter break and lacking my supervision, they could seriously hurt each other without intervention. I don't want any of you saddled with the task of disciplining them, so other than me remarrying within the next 24 hours, I'm out of ideas. Anyone?"

Everyone laughed uncomfortably.

Brittany, the new female guard, answered quickly. "You could hire a nanny for them. I have some contacts who may know-"

There was a knock on the door, and Hank said, "Sorry Brittany, one sec," then yelled "Come in."

It was Theo. "The staff is here, dad. Waiting for you to let them off the bus."

"Thanks Theo," said Hank kindly as he walked over and ruffled his son's hair. "Go ahead and let them know they can come in, but to be quiet because we're having a meeting in here."

"You aren't going to greet them at the door?"

"How about you do it for me this time? I think you'd be really good at that. Shake everyone's hand and welcome them back, just like I do. Okay?"

"Yes, sir."

"Good boy. Remember to tell them to be quiet. Go on."

Theo shut the door, and Hank turned back around to his guards.

"A nanny is not a bad idea, but it's going to take months to find one and vet her. I think for now, though, one of you is going to have to volunteer to stand in for me for the next four weeks, just to keep them in line until I get home. I'm sorry this is so damned awkward for all of us."

"What if you took one of them to work each day?" asked Avery. "The other one couldn't do much trouble if he's home alone."

Brittany spoke up again. "I think taking them out of the house will help them stop focusing on antagonizing each other. But we should take them to soup kitchens, animal shelters, et cetera. Places that need volunteers. Keep 'em busy all day and do some good. It will be good PR for you to have your boys contribute to the community. Maybe even something like Habitat for Humanity, since Theo likes to build stuff."

The guards all started talking amongst themselves while Hank thought about this option.

"But security-wise, I don't know if that's going to work," he finally responded. "Talk about making more work for you guys, which is what I was trying to avoid."

"I don't mind it," was the general consensus of the guards after several more minutes of discussion.

Then, Avery again. "Just be aware you have them in public again, though. Which means, if they start fighting again, everyone will know it."

Hank made up his mind. "Then they'll do separate things. Focus on what they like to do rather than what works for both of them. Theo can do some kind of building thing, some kind of physical labor, and Floyd can work with kids or the homeless."

Brittany put it, "Or you could just ask them what they want to do. Have them research some good causes and make their own decision about it."

Hank nodded thoughtfully. "I think that's a good idea. Keep them busy all day long, separate from each other, all the way up until dinner time. Everyone ok with that? We'll do it for a couple weeks, until they're in school again. Then back to the old program. Thanks Brittany. Anything else? No? Okay. I better go take care of Theo, then. Poor kid's been waiting all day for his reckoning. See you all in the morning, bright and early."

Hank trudged up the stairs and stopped into the spare room, where he grabbed the paddle he had just used on Floyd for disobeying him in the car (after discovering he wasn't actually wearing a belt and didn't feel like going to find one). He took it with him into his study and reluctantly hit the intercom button to summon Theo.

CHAPTER FOUR

Urbanes Headquarters

Denver, CO

"Holy. Shit. You see the paper yet, Colbert?"

Colbert paused from stirring the sugar in his tea and turned around to peer over his shoulder.

"Hell no, I'm still half asleep. What now? Oh...... *holy shit* ."

They looked at each other, grinned, then read the article in full, twice, not quite believing the implications of the news. "Let me borrow that paper for a minute. Thanks."

Colbert practically bounced into his boss's office, only to find Harmon sitting down to study the exact same article. Damn. He could never beat him to the punch on anything.

"Close the door," Harmon grumbled, "and stop acting like you just won Miss America. It's unprofessional. Sit down."

Colbert felt like a bucket of ice water had been dumped over him all of a sudden. Harmon had that effect on people, but he had never gotten used to it after all these years. No one had, really. He clenched his fists and waited in silence for his boss to finish reading the article.

"So," Harmon said as he set the paper down. "Looks like the first seeds of mistrust have been sown. That didn't take long. Have you been in contact with Yannick again?"

"No, we agreed he should go radio silent for a few days. I have no idea whether or not he actually talked to Daven, but obviously something huge has happened, and you know I don't believe in coincidences."

"And Yannick never confirmed back whether this emergency line was legit or not?"

"No."

Harmon sat back in his chair and drummed his fingers on the table. "I need to know if he spoke to Daven. If the line is still active. Just a simple yes or no will do. I want to know if this" - he jabbed a finger at the newspaper - "is our work, or if they're imploding on their own because of something else."

"I will do my best."

"Also, speaking of statements...we need to talk about Janet. I know you don't want to go there yet, but we haven't said anything publicly about her murder. Are you ready to work on it?"

"Hell yes. I mean, yes. Already on it. First things first, we have to state that we're looking into exactly why she was on Seditionists' property at the time. That's the first thing I want to know, too, but we have to wait for the FBI to do the security footage review."

Harmon said nothing, just... *tap, tap, tap.*

"The first thing people are going to say is that the Seditionists would never be stupid enough to commit murder on their own property, no matter who the victim is. They're going to be saying it's random. Or, that she was a double agent and gotten taken out by one of us. And if we address that publicly, all kinds of questions are going to come up that we can't even start to put answers to yet."

...tap, tap, tap.

"So Zane and I are meeting in a minute to put together some kind of statement, which right now is basically we are investigating the circumstances that led to this tragedy and extend our heartfelt thoughts and prayers for Janet's family and friends . As soon as she's in the ground, though, her family is going to be coming after us for answers."

...tap, tap, tap.

Colbert took a deep breath, feeling dizzy from the implications of what he was about to say next.

"And you're *really* not going to like this, since there's no point in me keeping my suspicions quiet at this point. But I think we have to seriously consider the possibility that she really *was* a double agent. I mean, it's possible when you starting thinking hard enough about it. If so...we fucked up big time, and Bancroft is going to catch on pretty fast. If he hasn't already, that is."

...tap, tap, tap.

Harmon's phone rang, and he leaned over to look at the phone display. A call from...Los Angeles?

Seditionist Headquarters, Los Angeles

Same day

Hank Bancroft stood at the espresso machine in Daven's office, trying and failing to figure out how to work the damned thing. He stopped trying when he heard Daven's assistant talking on the stairs.

"Billie!" he shouted.

Oh god, what did I do? Billie wondered in panic as she exchanged startled glances with her co-workers. She ran up the last few steps and tossed her purse down on her chair, absurdly upset that she hadn't even put lipstick on yet. Damn it.

She hurried in and looked around the office, surprised to find her boss not present. He was usually - no, always, the first one in the office.

"Oh, the espresso machine. I'll get that for you, sir." She hurried up to the machine and hoped she could remember how to do it. Hank made her terribly nervous.

"Wait, first things first. Close the door. And don't call me sir."
Hank had walked away now and was staring out the windows
into the ocean, just like Daven always did when he was
thinking hard. There was a newspaper in his hand.

Billie froze. She had hardly ever spoken to Hank, and only a
few times one-on-one when he was looking for Daven and
needed her help in tracking him down. Those few times, he
had always been very nice. Now...

Hank looked back and barked, "I said *close the door* . I need to
talk to you."

"Uh, yes, sir. Mr. Bancroft, I mean..." She was shaking, already
wondering if something terrible had happened to Daven. After
shutting the door, she leaned against it, back pressing hard
into it as if it could shield her from anything bad coming her
way.

Hank unfolded the paper and then turned around to lay it out
on the desk.

"Have you seen this yet?"

"No, sir."

"Hank."

"Hank." It sounded strange on her tongue. No one called him Hank, even when he wasn't around. Except for Rupert and Daven, of course, and Hank's assistant.

"Okay," he said, his tone softening considerably. "I'm sorry for being short with you. But I have news you need to hear immediately, before anyone else, because they're all going to come up to you for answers and gossip. And I need to make sure you are armed with a proper response."

"Is he alright?" Billie blurted before she could stop herself, the increasing fear of hearing that Daven had died overtaking her usual discretion.

Hank looked at her sideways. "Are you going to stay calm and listen to me, or-"

"Yes, sir."

Hank sighed, deciding not to worry about the 'sir' thing for the present.

"Billie, he violated a major policy and I had to suspend him. Rupert, too, but I'll talk to Ellen about him separately. It's already in the papers because I gave the government a heads-up yesterday, but we haven't made an official statement yet. Are you following?"

Billie nodded.

"Okay. People are going to start asking you questions the moment you find out. The exact statement you are going to make no matter who asks - and I mean *no matter who* - is 'I'm aware of the matter but not authorized to discuss it with anyone outside of Hank's leadership.' Repeat that, please."

"I'm aware of the matter but not authorized to discuss it with anyone outside of Hank's leadership team. Can I say Mr. Bancroft, though?"

"Yes, of course. Repeat it one more time."

Billie did, and he had her repeat it again for good measure. She was much calmer now.

"Okay. I want you to keep doing your job as if Daven was still here, but per the terms of our charter he is not allowed to contact anyone in the party until January 25. He will not contact you, and you're not to contact him. For any reason, I don't care what it is. Same goes with Rupert, although he'll be back on January 11. If you have any questions, ask me."

Billie swallowed hard. "I do have a question, sir. What did Daven do?"

She had a right to know, Hank knew, even as he hesitated. More so than probably anyone else who didn't already know.

"This stays between us. He missed a few calls to the emergency line, and then spoke to an unverified asset, all of which ended up causing a shit show that we're going to spend the few next months cleaning up. Rupert also spoke to the same unverified caller. I really don't know what got into either of them, but all I can say is this happened at my Christmas party, and you know what that was like."

The vast amount of alcohol and good cheer could have clouded their judgment, he meant. Daven didn't drink, as they both knew, but she let it be.

"Yes. I see what you mean. When are we going to make an official statement?"

"In a few hours." Hank was speaking to her much more kindly now, and he regretted having been so rude to her earlier.

"Look, I know how much you care about Daven, and vice versa. Just know I had absolutely no choice but to suspend them. They're lucky they weren't fired on the spot. It sucks, but we can't fall apart over this. Our constituents will depend on us to keep on going, business as usual."

Billie nodded, her expression determined and calm. "Ellen is most likely here by now. You should go talk to her right away."

Hank laughed; in two minutes Billie had gone from being petrified and calling him sir, to outright ordering him around. Learning fast.

"Yes ma'am," Hank said with a cheeky grin as he sprang up to open the door for her.

Billie almost died from embarrassment for a few minutes. But then she went in the bathroom to put on her lipstick, and cried her heart out for Daven.

After speaking to Ellen, who didn't take the news as hard as Billie had, Hank locked himself in his office and stared at all the papers Rupert and Daven had left on his desk for him.

The resignation letters, in particular. He should have accepted them. Anyone else would. Why didn't he?

Fuck.

He shoved them aside, then picked up the phone make a very difficult call.

Urbane Headquarters - Denver

"Hank *Bancroft*?" asked Harmon, a bit stunned.

"Yes, it's me. Don't act so surprised, we just talked like a week ago. I need a minute. Are you alone?"

Harmon looked up at Colbert, who shook his head. "Actually, no. I have Colbert with me. Just the two of us. Would you like me to send him out?"

"No. You're going to tell him what I have to say, anyway. Listen, I'm sure you've seen our little fiasco in the papers this morning, but that's not what I'm calling about."

"Okay. Then what-"

"The murder in Colorado on Christmas morning. It took place on Seditionists property, as you know. I want to review the surveillance footage as soon as possible, but I'm being told the FBI is going to give it to you first, and that you will then hand it over to us *at your leisure.*"

"Yes, of course. Our investigation should come first. She was *our* employee." Harmon was staring in confusion and alarm at Colbert, who shrugged back at him.

"I know that. If you're willing, however, the FBI will release copies to us both at the same time once they're done reviewing. You have to grant permission for that, so I'm faxing you the letter to sign and send over to us."

Sure enough, they immediately heard the *beep! OOOEEEEEE! WEOWEOWEOWEO!* of the fax machine under the desk. Harmon shook his head at Hank's bravado, then remembered Hank was actually on the phone and couldn't see the gesture. So he waited in annoyance for the fax machine to finish its ministrations before speaking again.

"And why would I want to do that, Hank?"

"Because a woman was murdered and it's only fair we both launch our investigations at the same time to get it resolved as quickly as possible and figure out who did this for the benefit of her family. I'm willing to take the fall for it if it was one of mine. And you should be equally willing if it was one of yours."

"So this is basically a PR move."

"Not my main aim, but yes, that too. Look, Harmon, I've got a lot of shit going on right now and have lost my two closest allies literally overnight. I have no ulterior motive here but to get this murder investigation going quickly. But since you're resisting, I'm going to make a very clear threat, and I don't care who knows about it. Hell, I'll tell the world myself. If you don't sign the form, I will personally inform Janet's family that you are not cooperating with the investigation by allowing us to immediately review the tapes to help identify her murderer, which could very well be someone from my own damned party. More likely yours, but that's not the point. Up to you where we go from here. I mean, I wouldn't want anyone to think you're *hiding* something. Do you?"

Checkmate. *Fuck*. Hank was a master. And really, Harmon had already known he was going to lose this battle as soon as it had begun. When Bancroft set his mind to something, he usually got it.

No. *Always* got it.

"I don't have the tapes yet, Hank. But when I do, I'll sign the form."

"No, you'll sign it now. I heard it come in, so I expect it back by end of the day, which means 5pm. Your time zone or mine, I don't care which."

Click.

Colbert didn't want to look at Harmon for fear of seeing him implode on the spot.

But Harmon said nothing. Just...*tap, tap, tap...*

CHAPTER FIVE

Hank Bancroft, leader of the Seditionists Party, confirmed today that he has placed two of his top executives on temporary unpaid leave per standard procedure. On December 26, Daven Johansson, Chief Strategist; and Rupert Aster, SVP Public Relations, reported to Mr. Bancroft that they had inadvertently violated an unspecified internal communications protocol for two phone calls made on December 24 and 25. As the communications involved non-strategic and public knowledge, the executives were allowed to remain after agreeing to a re-training program and reduction in salary. The Seditionists have always held all employees to rigid but fair standards and will continue to do so in the future.

Hank had spent at least two hours staring at the statement Rupert sent him for approval. He hated that it wasn't the truth. Transparency was one of his biggest obsessions, but it wasn't always possible. It felt wrong, but there was no one he truly trusted to bounce it off of for a second opinion. Or third, rather.

Except for Daven. Hank had been resisting the urge to call him all morning long. He missed his right hand man more than he would ever dare to admit. But he was giving in, against his will. Slowly.

Half an hour later, the battle was lost. He picked up the phone and quickly dialed the number that had always been so familiar and comforting. And strangely it still was, despite the circumstances.

"Hello Hank," replied the gruff, sleepy voice. Hank had woken him up. At 11am. That was strange.

"Hey, Dav. You awake? Do you have a minute?"

"Yes, and yes." He sounded wary and suspicious.

"I don't want to fight. Our media statement is due in an hour and I'm really not happy with it. Need your thoughts, if you're willing."

"Of course."

Hank read the statement to him, only realizing afterwards that part of it would be surprising and unhappy news for Daven. He hadn't meant to tell him this way, but it was too late now.

"Shit...we haven't talked about some of this yet. The salary and the re-training parts. I should have told you first."

Pause. "That would have been a better way, yes."

"Sorry. I wasn't thinking. If you're really not okay with this in any way, tell me now."

"Do I have a choice?" replied Daven coolly.

Hank cleared his throat, a bit unsettled by his own thoughtlessness and Daven's edgy replies. It was very unlike him, but Hank probably deserved it.

"Ok. I'm truly sorry, I'm an idiot. But let's stay on topic. What do you think about the statement?"

"Let's just say I completely understand why you're not comfortable with it. Too much spin."

"Yeah. But Rupert thinks we're exposing ourselves to some seriously bad press if we don't spin this enough. He's still pissed about my edits to the last release."

Daven asked Hank to read it again, so he did. Then Daven replied, "Rupert's right, though. You can't tell the whole truth all the time."

Hank couldn't stop himself from firing a bitter shot across Daven's bow . "Yeah. You've had a lot of experience with that one lately, huh?"

Silence from Daven. Hank didn't feel bad about the jibe. At all. There were more where that came from.

"Look," he continued after a moment, "I just can't put this statement out and then sit there through interviews repeating these outright lies. You guys may have no problem with it, but I have a conscience. It's not right, and it's not sustainable.

Daven still said nothing,

"You still there?"

"Yeah. It's funny that you're worried so much about transparency and honesty when you can't even bother to just say how you really feel, instead of hiding behind all this passive aggressive commentary. It's blatantly hypocritical, don't you think?"

Hank was so surprised at this blistering broadside that he actually thought he hadn't heard the man correctly. It took a minute for his brain to process the words and understand their meaning. Such open hostility had never passed between them before. Anger, yes, but nothing even remotely close to this. It hurt.

"You don't want to know how I really feel, Dav," was all he could say. A horribly weak response.

"You're correct, I don't. So let's get back on topic, as you said, and revise this statement so I can go back to bed. I have a suggestion on how to start it off…"

Harmon jumped as his fax machine started whirring and beeping again, and it seemed to take an eternity for the paper to spit itself out. He breathed a deep sigh of relief when he recognized Umber's number as the sender. It was a copy of an unusually lengthy press release from the Seditionists, with a handwritten note on the top.

King Hank the Oversharer strikes again! Game changer.

He smiled to himself. Hank had to approve that, so he could take it for granted that every single word of the oversharing masterpiece was the truth. But that didn't meant it was the whole story, either. December 24 and 25. So Yannick must have reached either one or both of them through the emergency line, and whatever they did about it (or didn't do) seems to have pissed Hank off royally. Especially Daven, apparently. And Hank hit them really hard in the wallet, too. Ouch.

So they were rattled, then. That was good. Very good.

But it wasn't a game changer. Yet.

CHAPTER SIX

As soon as the press release was out, Hank called Floyd to let him know he was ready to take him for his driving test.

"Where are you guys right now?" he asked tiredly.

"At the animal shelter but we're ready to go."

"Which animal shelter?" Hank asked, embarrassed that he had lost track of his kids. He had no idea where Theo was at all, come to think of it.

"The Santa Monica Humane Society. It's like ten blocks from the DMV."

"Okay. I'll call my driver now and meet you there at 1pm."

Floyd replied, "No, you took the Thunderbird to work so you have to drive it here."

"Oh yeah." Hank rubbed his temples. God, this headache.

"And did you remember to buy Shane lunch?"

Hank paused, completely puzzled by the unexpected question. "Did I what?"

"Buy Shane lunch. Yesterday on the phone, you said you would. Because you forgot about him."

Shit. Hank would have remembered on any other day, or made certain to send himself a reminder. He hated how scatterbrained he was feeling lately.

"Floyd, I'm going to have to hire you as my secretary if you keep this up."

Floyd laughed a little, not sure if it was a joke or not. "I don't think you could pay me enough for that," he replied carefully, hoping the humor wouldn't miss the mark.

Hank laughed, surprising even himself. It was amazing how nice it felt to laugh again. Without Dav and Rupert in the office to keep him constantly entertained, the day had felt like the world's longest funeral so far, and it was only noon.

"Probably not. I'll go see Shane now, then drive the Thunderbird to the DMV. See you soon. I love you, Floyd."

"Love you too, dad."

Hank had Vance drive the Thunderbird while he followed as a passenger in the SUV, stretched out in the back seat. It was nice to be able to indulge for once and hide behind the tinted windows, especially knowing full well the press statement was making its rounds and things were about to get out of control. The last vestiges of peace, and all that.

Of course word had gotten out that Floyd was taking his test today, so the parking lot at the DMV was filled with eager paparazzi who had become so emboldened over time that they openly stood there with their huge cameras and kept each other updated on Hank's movements. Driving a noisy old Thunderbird around town wasn't exactly the most discreet mode of transportation, and everyone got really excited when they heard it coming.

Groaning, Hank slumped even further into the seat and watched carefully as they meandered through the lot to see if the photographers were out for blood after having read the press release. It wasn't clear if they knew, though. Everything seemed normal. No one was overly excited, so maybe they hadn't seen it yet. Good.

Lucas pulled up to Avery's SUV so that the two identical cars were nearly touching, and Floyd rolled down the window to talk to his dad.

"You ready, Floyd? Big day, but you've got this," said Hank encouragingly.

"No. What are all these people doing here? I can't...I don't want to."

"It's okay. They want to see you succeed, too. Don't be afraid."

Floyd quickly clambered out the window and across the gap into the other car, flopping into Hank's lap before he could stop him. Not that he wanted to stop him, of course, but it wasn't exactly a dignified motion. The Thunderbird was parked directly in front of them and already surrounded by cameras being held by disappointed photographers. Nobody wanted pictures of the random driver. They wanted to see the Bancrofts.

Floyd was petrified at the sight of all the cameras clamoring for a shot of him, but Hank had expected them. The party's leader's son getting his driver's license was a big deal in the paparazzi world. Mostly because they wanted to be the first ones to know if Floyd failed, so they could gleefully spread the word. And Floyd knew it.

"Dad. Let's go home."

Hank shifted himself to a comfortable position and held his son like he was a small child, offering the kind of comfort that most boys stopped needing when they turned Theody's age. Neither of his sons were cuddlers at any age, so these moments were few and far between, and a lump soon appeared in Hank's throat that made it difficult to say anything for the moment.

"I don't want my license," Floyd said a few minutes later, his anxiety increasing to levels that would soon be uncontrollable if Hank didn't act fast. "Please. Can we just go home?"

"No. I know that you're afraid of failing, but that's life. We have to take chances or we'll never grow. I'm going to give you a few more minutes to get yourself together, and then we're getting out together so you can do your test."

"But dad, they're going to follow me around the whole time! It's not fair. Why can't we just be normal and do things like this without the whole world wanting to watch and waiting for us to make a mistake?"

Hank didn't know what to say. Floyd had never complained before about being in the spotlight, so this was new. Stage fright, as it were. But then again, the spotlight had never focused on him alone before. And one thing was certain: Floyd was right; they would follow him around and be watching for him to fail. And no, it wasn't fair at all.

"Okay, Floyd. Let me up. I'm going to go talk to them."

"Too late. There's like a dozen people out there and now more are coming." Floyd was looking backwards over Hank's shoulder at the entrance to the parking lot.

"Avery!" Hank yelled at the other car. "Go block the driveway, please. I don't want anyone else coming in here."

"It's a public parking lot," Avery replied, puzzled at the request. "We can't just go-"

"Don't care. Block it anyway."

"Yes, boss. But we're going to get the police called on us."

"I'm sure we will. Go."

Hank watched as Avery drove off and positioned the ponderous piece of machinery directly across the gate to the parking lot, effectively cutting off all cars from entering. Thankfully, the exit was separate and one-way, but he still fully expected to get completely trashed by the press in the next day's papers for abusing his powers to make the lives of his constituents that much harder.

"Floyd, get off my lap. Come on."

"No."

Hank shoved him off, then exited out the driver's side back door. The cameras went completely nuts; there were about 20 photographers now. Hank stayed still to let them take pictures, and then he raised a hand. Everyone fell completely silent and attentive, as expected. He could never deny that it was nice to have that kind of power.

"Gentlemen. My son is here to take a driving test, and frankly, you're scaring the hell out of him. He's fifteen years old and has way too much pressure on him already. Now, he is going to get out of this SUV in a moment and get into that

Thunderbird, and drive away with the instructor. Every single one of you who walks away right now without taking a single picture or leaving this parking lot until he gets back will receive a personal invitation from me to attend a press conference today at 4pm. Front and second row seats. Trust me, it's one you don't want to miss."

He turned around and pulled open the door as the men all murmured excitedly among themselves.

"Dad...no."

"It's alright, son. Come out. I've got you." He kept his voice loud enough so the photographers could hear him and hopefully have enough sympathy to keep their damned cameras from snapping every 2 seconds.

"No." Floyd moved away into the back row, out of Hank's reach. There was nothing Hank could do but drag him out, and he wasn't about to do that in front of the entire world. He had to think of something, fast, before they became a laughingstock. He turned back to the photographers.

"Alright, new plan. Everyone who wants to go to the presser needs to set down their cameras down on the ground - right here in front of me - and get back in their cars and stay put. This kid is not coming out until you do that, trust me. So either you get no pictures at all, or you get no pictures and an invitation. Your choice."

There was hesitation, and for one frightful moment Hank thought they were going to refuse en-masse. That would have been extremely embarrassing considering his position. But then...one man set his camera down, and that was all it took. The rest quickly followed, but then they all just stood there, looking dumbfounded.

"Into your cars, gentlemen," Hank snapped authoritatively. "Quickly, if you please. I'll let you know when you can get back out."

They turned away. Hank was keeping a careful eye on Avery's SUV; a line of cars was piling up to get in the lot and all the horns were starting to attract way too much attention to the group.

Hank poked his head back into the car.

"Floyd. *Out*. Right now. Your instructor is here and doesn't have all day."

"I'm scared," he said in a small voice, looking about 8 years old all of a sudden.

"No need. Nobody's going to follow you. I have all their cameras right here. Look. You got to go now, before more show up."

"I know, but..." He seemed about to refuse for good, then suddenly got a spurt of bravado and jumped out of the car. Hank looked around. There was a small crowd, but no one was taking photos. He pulled Floyd into a tight hug and then sent him off with a pat on the shoulder.

"If you don't pass, it's not the end of the world. Just do your best. Good luck."

"Thanks," said Floyd as he climbed into the driver's side. Then they were gone, and Hank let out the breath he'd been holding as he walked over to Vance.

"Nice one, boss," the man said with a huge smile.

"Yeah. Except now I got to invite these idiots to the office." His attention broke away as a man who obviously worked for the DMV came towards the group. All three guards jumped out of the SUV and went to Hank's side.

"Can I help you?" Lucas asked the man rudely, but Hank shushed him.

"I'm sorry we're blocking the driveway," Hank said apologetically. "We'll get him moved right away."

"Thank you, Mr. Bancroft, but I didn't come out here for that."

"Oh? How may I help you, then?"

"Just need to collect the $115 for your son's driving test. It was supposed to be paid over the phone ahead of time, but we can do it here." He held up a bulky credit card reader machine.

Hank flushed ten shades of red as he pulled out his wallet. "Of course. My apologies."

"No worries." The man worked busily at his task while Hank waited patiently. His guards all suddenly turned away, and Hank could see their shoulders quivering with laughter.

When it was done and Hank signed the receipt, he shook the man's hand and made some cheerful small talk, then promised again to move the SUV. The guards then pulled themselves together and were able to look at Hank again without cracking up.

Hank crossed his arms and glared at them. "Stand at attention. I ought to fire the lot of you right here and now. If he had pulled out a gun and held it to my head, no one would have noticed because you were too busy giggling like girls at a slumber party. Totally unprofessional. You're all docked today's pay. Fall out."

He turned away, waved to Avery to move out of the driveway, and climbed back in the SUV. He was furious at his guards, yes, but also at himself for being unable to see the humor in the situation. In the past, he would have been the one laughing the hardest. He had never docked any guard's pay before, either, and already regretted doing it.

God damn you, Daven.

His phone rang very loud in the silent car. The guards hadn't gotten back in yet, and he was glad for it.

"What's up, Taylor?"

"Shit's starting to hit the fan, boss. Your phone hasn't stopped ringing for the past twenty minutes or so. We're all going nuts here."

"I'm sure. Everything set for the 4pm presser?"

"Yeah. Who are we letting in?" Taylor was rapidly pounding on her keyboard.

"Got about twenty photographers in mind, so reserve the first two rows for them. I'll give you their names shortly. Open up the rest of the auditorium to first come, first serve."

"We did that once and people trampled each other trying to get in. You said we'd never do it again."

Hank shrugged. "These are new days, Taylor."

"I think it's a really bad idea, Hank. And it's my job to tell you when I think you have a bad idea."

"Noted. Then give them a numbered card as they pull in the parking lot. Once we reach one hundred, every single car after that gets turned away, period."

"But then we can't control who we're letting in and the room could end up dominated by Urbanes. And the questions you're going to get..."

Hank didn't feel like fighting about this. "They have a press card, they can come in. End of story. Last thing: I don't want any of the questions to be plants. I'm not going to let it be said that we packed the room with our own people in order to avoid uncomfortable questions. Are you going to argue about that, too?"

"No."

"Good. Get this info out on the wires ASAP."

"Okay, boss. It's your show."

"Yes it is. Thank you for remembering that."

He hung up the phone, his irritation with himself increasing by the second, and sat in the car for twenty more minutes, leaning back against the headrest with his eyes closed in order to help stave off the horrific headache that was growing worse in proportion to the number of things he began worrying about.

Hank desperately wanted to talk to Daven. But he also never wanted to talk to him again. He picked up his phone, hoping to see a missed call from the man. Nothing. Of course. Maybe he was still asleep, and would call when he woke up.

Avery poked his head inside the car, jerking Hank out of his very dark thoughts.

"They're coming back, sir."

Hank got out of the car and waited as the Thunderbird pulled up to his feet and parked. As he crossed in front of it Floyd leaned on the horn, startling him out of his wits. Floyd's favorite prank. Hank should have known better.

He broke into a huge grin. "Hey bud. Thanks for the heart attack. How'd you do?"

"I passed, dad!"

"Awesome!" They hugged, and Hank shook the instructor's hand.

"He was flawless, Mr. Bancroft. Not a single point off."

"Good. Hop in with Avery, Floyd. We'll celebrate tonight."

Then, to Lucas. "We'll drive away first with Avery, and Vance can take the Thunderbird. Can you walk around and get the business cards from these guys, and tell them to come retrieve their cameras? Then call Taylor ASAP and give her all the names and numbers from the cards."

"Yes, sir."

"Thank you."

Lucas said quickly, "Sir, I'm really sorry about what happened. We all feel pretty terrible about it."

"Good. That means it won't happen again, then."

Lucas nodded and headed towards the cameras. Hank pulled out his phone, turned the ringer off, and put it back in his pocket as he climbed in beside Floyd.

"Want to swing through Dairy Queen on the way home?"

"Yeah!"

"Avery-"

"This car doesn't fit in their drive-thru, boss. We can hit the Shake Shack, though."

"Shake Shack it is, then. Tell me about the test, Floyd."

His son was beaming up at him, chatting away excitedly, and Hank slid his arm around him and relaxed into the seat.

Floyd was happy, and nothing else mattered right now.

CHAPTER SEVEN

Hank was well aware he should return to the office sooner than he was planning to, but there was no use in rushing back just to sit as his desk alone and be depressed again. But he did need to make Floyd pause for breath for a moment while he made a quick call.

"Hey Taylor. Can you check my fax machine and see if..." he looked at Floyd, knowing he would likely be highly disturbed by any mention of Harmon. "You know, that fax we are expecting by 5pm. Has it arrived yet?"

"One sec."

Hank patted Floyd's leg. "You ate that fast," he said, indicating the double waffle cone that was now dripping all over the place. "Going to have a sugar rush."

"So are you."

"Ha. True." Hank had been so distracted by Floyd's chatter that he didn't notice (or taste) the root beer float he had inhaled in the short time it took to get back to the house. There was a Federal Express truck out front. It must be delivering Daven's memo. Was he home now, or was he visiting Rupert? *Of course he was home. Where else would he be, anyway? It's not like he had any friends.* Except for Rupert. *You know, because he's literally given up his entire life to work for you.* They could be together right now, talking about him. Saying who knows what?

Maybe even agreeing they don't want to come back to work for me.

"Hank? Hank?" prompted Taylor into his ear.

"Oh. Sorry, bit of a bad connection."

"Nothing yet."

"What?" He'd actually forgotten what he called her about, to his chagrin.

"The fax. I can hear you fine, by the way. I think we should move the press conference to 5pm."

"Why?" Hank asked in a quizzical tone.

"Because that's how long you gave Harmon to respond to the fax. What if he doesn't do it until 4:59pm? Then you've lost a prime opportunity to put some serious pressure on him."

Hank smiled. "This is why you're my right hand man, Taylor."

"Only for now. So that's a yes?"

"Yes," Hank replied, swallowing hard at the jibe. He had always thought of Taylor that way. Maybe he should tell people how he felt about them more often. "Move it and announce it ASAP. Thanks kiddo. You're doing a great job. See you in a bit." He hung up and turned to his son.

"Floyd, do me a favor. Pull the Thunderbird into the garage. I'll take the SUV back to work. Come to think of it…I think I heard a rattle, so you may need to drive it around the block a few times first just to make sure it's running okay."

"A rattle? From where?" Floyd was instantly concerned, but then he saw the mischievous sparkle in his dad's eye and he grinned. "Right. I'll make sure to check it out. Drive it around for a while."

"Ten minutes should do the trick," said Hank firmly. "Absolutely no main streets. *Ten minutes*, tops."

He handed the keys to his delighted son, then hopped out and walked around to Avery's window.

"Follow Floyd around, then come back and get me. I gave him ten minutes, and if he goes on a main street let me know so I can kill him when he gets home."

"Got it, boss."

Hank patted the window frame, then walked up to the house to intercept the FedEx delivery man at the front door, even though his butler was already there to take the delivery.

"I got this, Maurice. Thanks."

He signed for the envelope and then took it into his study. It had to be the report that Daven had sent him yesterday to prove he and Rupert were reporting themselves voluntarily and not as a result of Shane's findings. Hank hadn't yet read the copy of the memo yet, so this was a new, fresh wound that he didn't want to reopen already.

Re-open? Actually, it was still gaping wide. It might never *not* be fresh. There might never be enough healing. The scars would never fade, if they ever formed at all.

God help me...

He didn't have the courage to open it yet and threw the entire unopened envelope into his locking drawer. Then he picked up his secure phone line - the one that nobody could trace back to his home - and started dialing.

Urbanes Headquarters, Denver

"Sir, I have a call for you from Shot One," announced the receptionist quietly over the secure intercom line.

Harmon's head jerked up from the new dress code policy he had been approving. Or rather, not approving. Dealing with any amount of HR nonsense made him feel slightly homicidal. Even enough that a call from his main rival was a welcome distraction.

"Send Colbert in here first, then put it through."

His right hand man arrived and locked the door, then they both took deep breaths and sat down.

"Hello, Hank. Just for transparency's sake, I want to let you know Colbert is with me again."

"Good afternoon to you both. I'm told we haven't received your fax yet."

"Yeah. It's not 5pm. Impatient, are we? Makes me wonder why."

Hank smiled to himself as he picked up a framed photo of himself and Daven at Crater Lake. That was a fun trip, although all the water-skiing had taken a toll on his knees that he hadn't quite recovered from yet. And Daven…he had gotten all drunk and giggly from just two cans of beer and then insisted on busting out the karaoke machine. Rupert was never going to let him forget it for as long as they all lived.

"Not impatient at all," Hank responded pleasantly. "Just concerned that it didn't come through. We're moments away from announcing a press conference at 5pm Pacific, and questions about Janet might come up. I'm just hoping by then to have some guidance on what you would like me to say about the matter, just to ensure we are on the same page."

In other words: *send me the fax, you fucker, or I'll throw you under the bus faster than you can say 'constituent mutiny.'*

"I see," Harmon responded slowly. Tap. "Is this a live broadcast, then?"

"Yes, with a press audience. Your reporters are welcome. There will be a Q&A. I'm really looking forward to being able to say whatever I want, since Rupert isn't around to dictate my every word and slap my hand for saying too much. You know how I can be sometimes."

Tap. Tap. "Silly me. For a moment I thought you were making another threat. Obviously I'm completely wrong, because you would never stoop so low. I would very much appreciate the opportunity to be educated on what your motives are right now, if you would be so kind. Just to 'ensure we are on the same page,' as you said."

"Allow me to offer my apologies," Hank responded politely. "It appears I'm the one who is jumping to conclusions this time by thinking you're trying to somehow slow down the speed of the investigation. I would also appreciate the opportunity to be educated on *your* motives. You know I've always valued the chance to learn something new from you, as rare as that may be.”

God damn, breathed Colbert as he eyed his boss warily. How the hell did Hank Bancroft even manage to walk around with balls that size? If he didn't hate him so much, he would admire him.

“Apology accepted, Hank,” Harmon responded coolly, after he had taken a moment to gather his wits. “As planned, the fax will come to you at 3pm when my secretary returns from lunch.”

“Oh she's already back, I just talked to her. Nice girl, seems efficient. I'm sure she can take care of this for you in no time.”

Harmon looked about ready to implode, but he kept his tone even. “Thank you for letting me know. But again, as I said, you will receive a fax at 3pm. Oh, and please extend my congratulations to your son for passing his driving test. We were all rooting for him, you know, even if he does misbehave in church. I'm certain he was properly disciplined and it won't happen again. Goodbye, Hank.”

Click. Harmon slammed down the phone and then looked up at Colbert with a dangerous gleam in his eye.

"That fucker! I swear to god, if I ever win an argument with him I might just have a stroke from the shock of it. What do you think he's really up to?"

"I told you. I think Janet was a double agent and he's catching on. And now, after this…I'm almost sure of it."

"*Almost sure* ? No such thing. You're either sure, or you're not. Can't have it both ways."

Colbert said nothing. Once Harmon began to fight about semantics, he was too rattled to reason with any further. Anyone who had brains dared not argue with him under such circumstances.

Tap. Tap. Tap.

www.ingramcontent.com/pod-product-compliance
Lightning Source LLC
Chambersburg PA
CBHW060558100726

47907CB00005B/1429